MY NAME IS
York

written by

ELIZABETH VAN STEENWYK

illustrated by

BILL FARNSWORTH

rising moon

www.northlandpub.com

For my sons, Matthew and Brett: scouts, explorers, and friends. —E. V. S.

For my wife, Deborah, and my daughters, Allison and Caitlin. — B. F.

Bill Farnsworth would like to give special thanks to Dan Freeman and Maurice Jajer.

www.northlandpub.com

The illustrations were rendered in oils on linen
The text type was set in Truesdell
The display type was set in Nuptial

Composed in the United States of America
Manufactured in Hong Kong

FIRST HARDCOVER IMPRESSION, June 1997
FIRST SOFTCOVER IMPRESSION, September 1999

04   05   7

ISBN 0-87358-758-8 (pb)

Library of Congress Cataloging-in-Publication Data
Van Steenwyk, Elizabeth.
My name is York / written by Elizabeth Van Steenwyk ; illustrated
by Bill Farnsworth.
p. cm.
Summary: A Slave describes the journey he makes with his master,
Captain William Clark, into the uncharted territory of the American
West to find a water passageway to the Pacific Ocean.
1. Lewis and Clark Expedition (1804–1806)—Juvenile fiction.
{1. Lewis and Clark Expedition (1804–1806)—Fiction. 2. West
(U.S.) —Discovery and exploration —Fiction. 3. Afro-Americans —
Fiction.} I. Farnsworth, Bill, ill. II. Title.
PZ7.V358Mp 1997
{E}—dc21   97-8816

Foreword

THIS IS THE STORY of one man's dream for a nation and another man's dream for himself. In 1803, President Thomas Jefferson wanted to expand this country's boundaries. First, he asked Congress to buy a great portion of land west of the Mississippi River, then owned by France. This was carried out in an act called the Louisiana Purchase, which doubled the area of the United States. Then he wanted that land explored in order to find a water passageway to the Pacific Ocean. This passage would help to establish a trade route from one ocean to the other for the young nation.

Jefferson decided to send Captains Meriwether Lewis and William Clark on this exciting journey of discovery. Lewis had experience in military and frontier life, and had been Jefferson's private secretary. He chose Clark, another military man, to act as co-leader of the group. Their expedition became one of the most important that the nation had ever undertaken. It filled out the map of the United States from coast to coast, and later Jefferson said it "substituted knowledge for dreams."

When Europeans began their explorations of the western hemisphere, they needed laborers to do the physical work of cultivating the land they claimed. Europeans began the practice of bringing African slaves to North and South America early in the seventeenth century.

York, a black slave belonging to Captain Clark, accompanied his owner on the trip and brought his dream with him. Like all slaves everywhere, York dreamed of being a free man.

The boats slip into the water at dawn and the journey begins. Some people think we may find monsters out West. But our leaders, Captain Lewis and Captain Clark, say that is an idea for dreamers. There is no room for dreaming on this journey into the unknown.

Still, I dream, and I carry my dream within me as we begin our quest to find a waterway to the western sea. I dream of finding freedom. My name is York and I am a slave. Although we have been lifelong companions, Captain Clark is still my master. He does not know that I have a quiet quest of my own.

The waters of this river run wide and swift as we put miles behind us. It throbs with strength against our poles. As we count passing days by making knots on rawhide thongs, the wilderness increases in determined fierceness along the shores. It hides the owners of curious eyes. Yet, we know someone is there, following our journey closely on silent feet.

We stop many nights for food and rest before the Indians step out to greet us with hands of friendship extended. It is with wonder that they approach me, and I, in turn, search their bronze faces. Strength and dignity respond. Soon, I will ask them if they know which way freedom lies.

At night we go to the Council House of our new friends and take places around the fire. Even Seaman, Captain Lewis's dog, finds his place and waits with anticipation. Their chief offers up a pipe of peace and points it toward the four corners of the earth and heavens.

Music begins from their tambourines made of hoops and skins. Deer and goat hooves, fastened to long poles, count the rhythm for Indian feet. One night later, we return and make music of our own with a fiddle and a horn. They marvel that so large a man as I can dance with such ease and skill.

Our journey continues until one morning we wake to measure our breath in small, white puffs. It is time, our leaders agree, to winter over.

Amid the lives of the Mandan tribe, we build cabins of cotton-wood logs. We pull our boats ashore as ice slows the river on its journey. One magical night we awaken to see the sky alive with columns of streaking stars. They tell me these are the Northern Lights, and I am awed by their radiance. For a moment, I forget that I am slave to Captain Clark as we stand together, two mortals awed by God's brilliance in His heaven.

Sacajawea, wife of Charbonneau the French trapper, is great with life within her. They join us on our journey. On a morning brittle with cold, she delivers a son. We rejoice in his health and newness. Which words will he choose to speak? Hidatsa, English, French, or all, as his parents do?

During the long days of winter, we sew breeches, shirts, and coats of elkskin. When we find signs of the large bear and emerge from our own hibernation, we look much alike. But inside my skin, I am different. My dream of freedom beats inside me, alone among these men and one woman.

Cottonwood trees send out fresh leaves, and plum bushes greet us in full bloom as we point our boats westward once more. Soon, we come to the River That Scolds All Others. We understand the Indian name as we listen to the river churn rapidly with the voice of a woman scolding her children, while smoothing stones to roundness in its bed.

Buffalo cast their shadow on the prairie now and Indian bands follow. Soon we encounter both and feast before we smoke the pipe of peace. Sioux and Shoshones respect our leaders, calling my master the Red-Headed Chief Whose Tongue Is Straight. He is fair, they say. Will my freedom be found in his fairness?

High plains and deep forests challenge us, and our bodies
strain against the work we endure to pass through them.
Mountains grow higher, gorges deeper, as we search for the
westward waterway. We pause to admire a great fall of water
that tumbles into white foam below.

Captain Clark explores a deep ravine with Sacajawea and
Charbonneau while I wait above to enjoy the warmth of sky
and sun.

Suddenly the sky darkens. Angry clouds release a torrent. I find shelter beneath a chalky overhang and then I remember: Captain Clark and the others have not returned.

I run to the cliff's edge and see their desperate struggle as water rises in the ravine. Sacajawea hands her small son to me. Then I reach out to her and Charbonneau. But where is Captain Clark?

Now he struggles upward too, before I reach out to pull him to safety. When he can speak, he tells me that his compass is lost. Later, he finds it and I wonder: Will that compass one day point my way to freedom?

We cross the Bitterroot Mountains where snow still drifts. Food grows scarce, but we share what we have with the Nez Perce and they with us. Sacajawea digs for wild artichokes, but there are few. We miss the abundance of plump chokecherries and greens that grew near the great falls.

Men, women, and children gather near me to touch my color and I, in turn, touch theirs. We marvel at our sameness. They begin to call me Great Medicine.

We pass through many canyons before arriving at a sagebrush plain. A river begins and we follow its growth along a tumbling course. Through high country it winds as rocks project into its current. Rapids create mighty hazards as we move ever west in tired boats.

Then we overcome a final thrust of mountains and there is the scent of ocean in the air. Soon we stand where water and land unite and rejoice in our success. We have found a waterway to the western sea. Captain Clark carves his name on a large pine.

"William Clark December 3 1805 By land from the U. States in 1804 and 1805." He carves the names of his men as well. I trace my fingers along my letters. I was here, it says. My name is York and I was here.

When spring returns, our thoughts turn homeward. Along the way our Indian friends set fire to large trees at night. This will bring us luck on our journey home, they say.

Surely, freedom is out there, somewhere, waiting for me.

Afterword

CAPTAIN CLARK never granted York his freedom. However, when the expedition ended, he gave York permission to go to Louisville, Kentucky, where he married. Clark also gave York a wagon and some horses so that he could enter the hauling business, by which he earned his living. Although York asked again and again for his freedom, Captain Clark never granted it legally.

York entertained friends with stories of his adventures on the expedition as long as he lived. He died of cholera in Tennessee.

It was not until January 1, 1863, almost 60 years after the expedition, that the Emancipation Proclamation freed all slaves, including York's descendants.

President Thomas Jefferson's vision of the nation's future was remarkable when he sent Meriwether Lewis and William Clark on their momentous journey across thousands of unknown miles to find a water passage to the Pacific. One of the most important voyages of discovery that the nation has ever undertaken, the Lewis and Clark expedition truly did substitute knowledge for dreams.

William Clark December 3 1805
By land from U. States in
1804 and 1805

Capt. Meriwether Lewis
York
Cha
Sac
T

About the Author and Illustrator

Elizabeth Van Steenwyk is the author of more than 50 books for young people and more than 250 articles and short stories for adult and children's magazines. She was born and grew up in Galesburg, Illinois, the hometown of Carl Sandburg, and graduated from Knox College with a B.A. in English. Her early career was spent writing for radio and television, with a concentration on children's programming. Elizabeth and her husband, Donald, have two grown sons and live in San Marino, California.

Bill Farnsworth is a graduate of The Ringling School of Art and Design and a member of the Society of Illustrators and the Air Force Art Program. He has illustrated nine children's books to date, including *The Buffalo Jump*, also from Northland Publishing.

Bill has been included with sixteen of the finest aviation artists in the country to produce paintings for the United States Air Force fiftieth-anniversary, limited-edition book and prints. He lives in Venice, Florida, with his wife, Deborah, and their daughters, Allison and Caitlin.